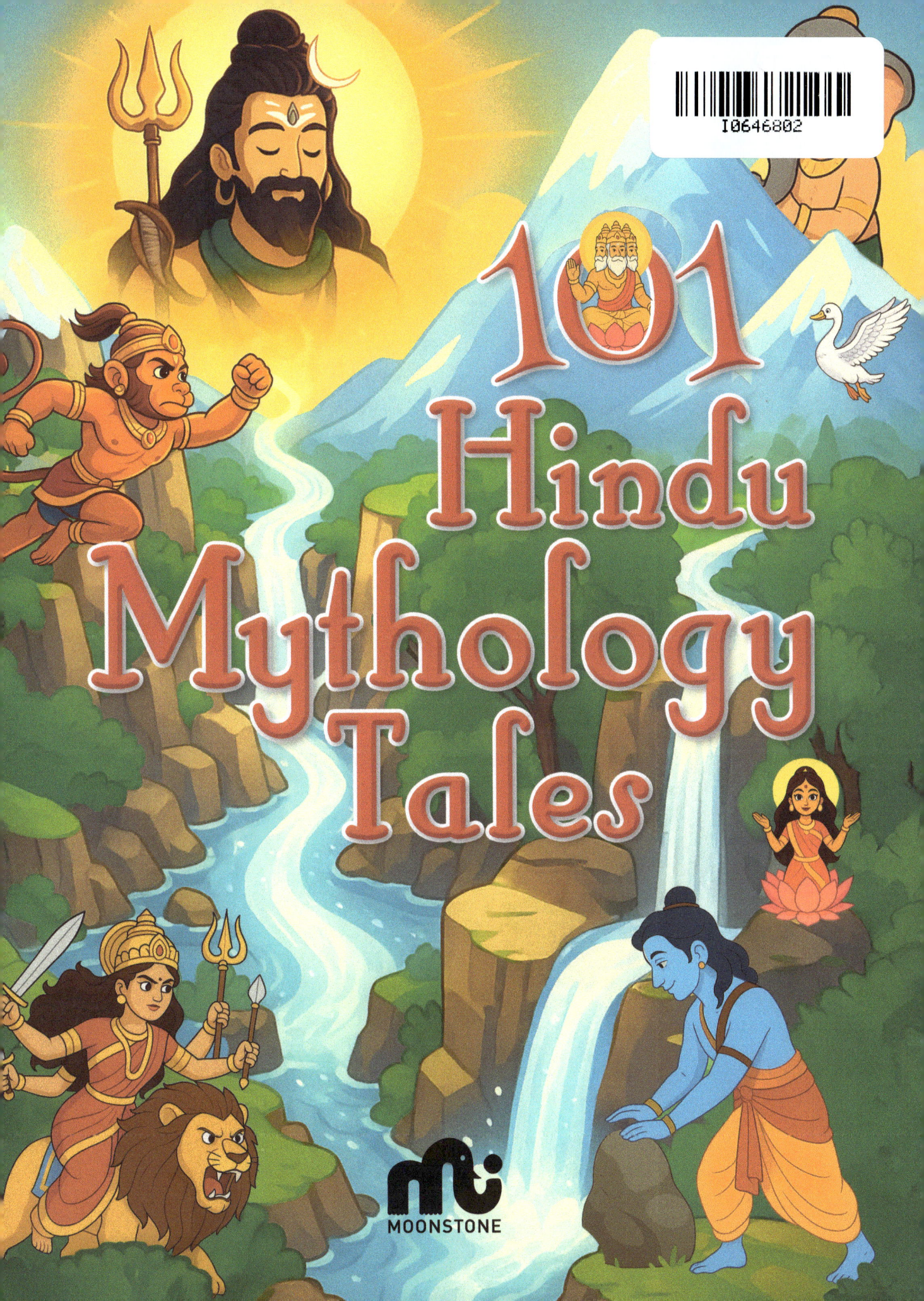

101 Hindu Mythology Tales

MOONSTONE

Published in Moonstone
by Rupa Publications India Pvt. Ltd 2025
7/16, Ansari Road, Daryaganj
New Delhi 110002

Sales centres:
Bengaluru Chennai
Hyderabad Jaipur Kathmandu
Kolkata Mumbai Prayagraj

P-ISBN: 978-93-7003-741-0
E-ISBN: 978-93-7003-786-1

First impression 2025

10 9 8 7 6 5 4 3 2 1

Contents

Contents

1. Shiva's Dance of Bliss

Once upon a time, Lord Shiva decided to perform his *Ananda Tandava*, a dance of pure joy. As he danced in the sacred city of Kashi, his movements shook the heavens and the earth. The stars twinkled, and the rivers sang. Shiva's dance created and destroyed everything in its path, reminding all the gods that life is a balance of creation, preservation, and destruction. The people of Kashi watched in awe, knowing they were witnessing the cosmic dance that ruled the universe.

2. The Theft of the Shiva Lingam

Long ago, the Demon King Ravana wanted the power of Lord Shiva's Jyotirlinga, which was kept safely in the temple at Ujjain. One night, he tried to steal it, but Lord Shiva had other plans. The moment Ravana tried to lift the lingam; it grew so heavy that his hands gave way. Ravana then tried to put it down, but the lingam sank deep into the earth, and it is said that it's still hidden underground, sending blessings to the city of Ujjain forever.

3. The Journey of Lord Jagannath

Every year, Lord Jagannath, along with his siblings, Balabhadra and Subhadra, take a journey to a nearby temple. This grand procession is called the *Rath Yatra*, where the three deities ride on huge chariots. Once, when they were about to embark on their journey, Lord Jagannath told the people that the journey was not just to the temple but to the hearts of all his devotees. Thousands of people follow the chariots, pulling them with love and devotion, as the gods bless them from above.

4. The Boon of Lord Venkateshwara

Long ago, Lord Venkateshwara, the god of wealth and prosperity, was meditating on the hills of Tirumala. A devotee named Akasa came and asked the Lord for a blessing. Lord Venkateshwara told him, "Whoever prays to me with a pure heart will receive everything they desire." Akasa prayed for many days and was blessed with wealth and wisdom. To this day, people come to Tirupati, seeking the Lord's blessings for a happy life and prosperity.

5. The Ganges Meets the Earth

Once, the mighty Ganges River flowed in the heavens, but the people of the Earth longed to bathe in her holy waters. To bring her down, the gods asked Lord Shiva for help. He agreed, but knowing her power, he caught the Ganges in his matted hair, softening her fall. As the river gently flowed down, it touched the Earth for the first time, blessing the land with purity and joy. Now, every year, people come to Rishikesh to dip into the Ganges and wash away their sins.

6. Krishna Lifts Govardhan Hill

One day, the people of Vrindavan were preparing for a grand feast to please Lord Indra, the god of rain. But young Krishna, seeing that the villagers were giving too much attention to Indra, asked them to instead honour the mountain Govardhan. Angered, Indra sent a terrible storm to punish the villagers. But Krishna, with a smile, lifted the entire mountain on his little finger, sheltering the villagers and cows from the rain. From that day, people celebrated Krishna as the protector of Vrindavan.

7. The Sinking of Lord Krishna's Kingdom

Lord Krishna once ruled the magnificent city of Dwaraka. It was a city filled with wealth, peace, and happiness. But one day, a curse was placed upon it, and it slowly sank into the sea. As the waters rose, Krishna called upon his friends and told them to leave the city before it vanished. The people of Dwaraka wept, but Krishna comforted them, assuring them that they would always be in his heart. Today, the ruins of Dwaraka lie beneath the waves, a reminder of Krishna's divine presence.

8. Hanuman's Mighty Leap

Long ago, the Monkey God Hanuman was sent on a mission to find the abducted Sita. When he reached the island of Lanka, he had to cross the vast ocean. With a smile, Hanuman grew in size and leapt across the sea in a single bound. His mighty leap shook the heavens, and as he landed, the ground trembled. Hanuman's devotion to Lord Rama and his strength became a legend, inspiring all who heard the story.

9. Kamakshi and the Demon

Once, the demon king Banasura wanted to marry the goddess Kamakshi. He trapped her in his palace, thinking she would obey him. But Kamakshi, with her pure heart, prayed to Lord Shiva for help. Shiva, moved by her devotion, appeared and destroyed Banasura's palace, freeing Kamakshi. She returned to Kanchipuram, where she became the protector of the city. To this day, people visit Kanchipuram, seeking her blessings for love and strength.

10. The Birth of Lord Rama

In the ancient city of Ayodhya, King Dasharatha and Queen Kausalya were blessed with a son, Lord Rama. From the moment he was born, it was clear that Rama was no ordinary child. He was the incarnation of Lord Vishnu, destined to defeat the evil demon king Ravana. Rama grew up to be a brave and wise prince, loved by all. His life, full of challenges and victories, teaches the values of duty, love, and righteousness.

11. The Birth of River Narmada

A long time ago, there was a goddess named Narmada, who lived in the Himalayas. She wanted to bring prosperity and fertility to the land below. One day, she prayed to Lord Shiva, who granted her the gift of flowing as a river from the mountains. As she descended, the gods sent her into a beautiful gorge, where her waters flowed through the land, giving life to all. The people of Bhedaghat still celebrate the goddess and the life she brought to the earth.

12. Lord Murugan Defeats the Demon Surapadman

In Tiruchendur, Lord Murugan, the son of Lord Shiva, fought the demon Surapadman, who had been terrorising the heavens. With his divine spear, Vel, Lord Murugan battled the demon for days, displaying great strength and valour. Surapadman, after a fierce battle, was finally defeated. To honour Murugan's victory, the people of Tiruchendur built a temple in his name. Every year, they celebrate his victory over evil, remembering his courage and determination.

13. Lord Shiva and the Poison

Long ago, the gods and demons churned the ocean to obtain the nectar of immortality. But a terrible poison, *halahala*, emerged instead. It threatened to destroy the universe. In a moment of great courage, Lord Shiva drank the poison to protect the world. His throat turned blue, and he became known as *Neelkanth*, the one with the blue throat. The gods praised him for his sacrifice, and since then, Lord Shiva has been worshipped as the protector of all.

14. Nataraja's Cosmic Dance

In Chidambaram, Lord Shiva performed his famous dance, the *Tandava*, which symbolises the creation and destruction of the universe. As he danced, the world around him transformed. Rivers flowed, mountains rose, and the sun and moon danced along with him. The celestial beings watched in awe, realising that through destruction, new life would come. This dance of Shiva continues to remind everyone of the cycle of life and the eternal rhythm of the universe.

13

15. The Story of Lord Shiva's Lingam

Once, the Pandavas, in their quest for redemption after the Kurukshetra war, sought Lord Shiva's blessing. They found him at Kedarnath, but Lord Shiva, wishing to avoid them, transformed into a bull and ran to

another place. However, the Pandavas were persistent, and Lord Shiva finally appeared before them, blessing them with peace. The famous Kedarnath temple was built to honour Shiva's presence, and the sacred lingam there is said to grant divine grace to those who visit.

16. The Story of Lord Vishnu's Boon

In the ancient city of Gaya, King Gaya once performed an intense penance to please Lord Vishnu. Pleased by the king's devotion, Vishnu appeared and granted him a boon. He asked for the ability to give peace to the souls of his ancestors. Vishnu, with his blessings, told the king that anyone who came to Gaya to perform rituals would have their ancestors' souls freed from the cycle of rebirth. Since then, people visit Gaya to perform *shraddha* and offer prayers for their ancestors.

17. The Story of Nara and Narayana

Long ago, two sages, Nara and Narayana, meditated in the forests near Badrinath. They were so devoted that they never left their spot, even during harsh winters. Pleased by their dedication, Lord Vishnu appeared before them and promised to stay in the region forever. Since then, Badrinath has become one of the most sacred places for Hindus, with Lord Vishnu in his form as Badrinath, continuing to bless all who come seeking his divine presence.

18. The Divine Birth of Vaishno Devi

In the hills of Katra, there once lived a beautiful and powerful woman named Vaishnavi. She was the incarnation of Goddess Durga, sent to rid the world of evil. When the demon king, Bhairon, tried to harm her, Vaishno Devi fled into the mountains. Bhairon followed her but was defeated by the goddess, who manifested her power. The place where this divine battle occurred is now home to the Vaishno Devi temple, where millions of pilgrims come each year to seek the goddess's blessings.

19. The Story of Amarnath Cave

Many years ago, Lord Shiva decided to reveal the secret of immortality to his wife, Parvati. He journeyed to the remote Amarnath cave to share this secret. However, a pair of pigeons overheard them and were blessed with immortality. To this day, the cave is believed to contain the divine ice Shiva Lingam, which is formed naturally every year. Pilgrims visit Amarnath in the summer months to seek blessings and glimpse the divine lingam.

20. The Story of Lord Rama's Worship

During the great battle with the Demon King Ravana, Lord Rama realised that he needed Lord Shiva's blessing to defeat Ravana. He built a temple at Rameshwar and prayed to Lord Shiva, offering his devotion. In response, Lord Shiva blessed him with strength and victory. Rama defeated Ravana, and after his victory, he worshipped Shiva at Rameshwar. To this day, Rameshwar is known for the powerful connection between Lord Rama and Lord Shiva, making it one of the holiest places for Hindus.

21. The Curse of Sage Bhrigu

Sage Bhrigu was once deep in meditation when he became angry with Lord Vishnu for not acknowledging him. In a fit of rage, he kicked Lord Vishnu in the chest. As a result, Lord Vishnu, with a calm demeanour, took the kick without retaliation. However, the goddess Lakshmi, Vishnu's consort, was deeply hurt and left him. Realising his mistake, Sage Bhrigu went to apologise, and Vishnu, with his infinite compassion, forgave him. This story teaches the importance of humility and the consequences of pride.

22. The Story of Ganesha's Birth

Goddess Parvati, feeling lonely while Lord Shiva was away, decided to create a son from the dirt of her body. She breathed life into him, and thus, Ganesha was born. When Shiva returned, he did not recognise Ganesha and, in a fit of anger, severed his head. Parvati was heartbroken, and Shiva, realising his mistake, promised to restore Ganesha's life. He sent his followers to bring the head of the first living creature they encountered, which happened to be an elephant. Ganesha was revived with the head of an elephant, and thus, he became the remover of obstacles.

23. The Story of King Bali and Vamana

King Bali was a powerful demon who ruled the three worlds. The gods, jealous of his power, sought help from Lord Vishnu. Vishnu incarnated as a small dwarf, Vamana, and asked Bali for three paces of land. Bali, being generous, granted the request. However, Vamana grew to a gigantic size and with three strides, covered all of Bali's kingdom. Realising that he had been outwitted, Bali humbly offered his own soul to Lord Vishnu. Vishnu granted him a place in the underworld, where Bali continues to rule, symbolising humility and selflessness.

24. The Story of the Snake and the Mongoose

Once, a kind woman had a pet mongoose that protected her home. One day, a venomous snake entered the house and tried to harm her baby. The mongoose fought the snake bravely and killed it, but when the woman returned, she saw the mongoose covered in blood and assumed it had harmed her baby. In a tragic misunderstanding, she killed the mongoose. When she discovered her mistake, she was heartbroken, realising that the mongoose had only tried to save her child. This story teaches the consequences of rash judgment and the importance of trust.

25. The Story of Dhruva's Devotion

Dhruva, a young prince, was deeply hurt when his father refused to let him sit on his lap, favouring his stepbrother. Determined to prove his worth, Dhruva left his kingdom and went into the forest to meditate, calling out to Lord Vishnu. After years of intense penance, Vishnu appeared and blessed him, granting him a place in the sky as the North Star. Dhruva's story teaches the importance of determination, devotion, and faith in overcoming obstacles.

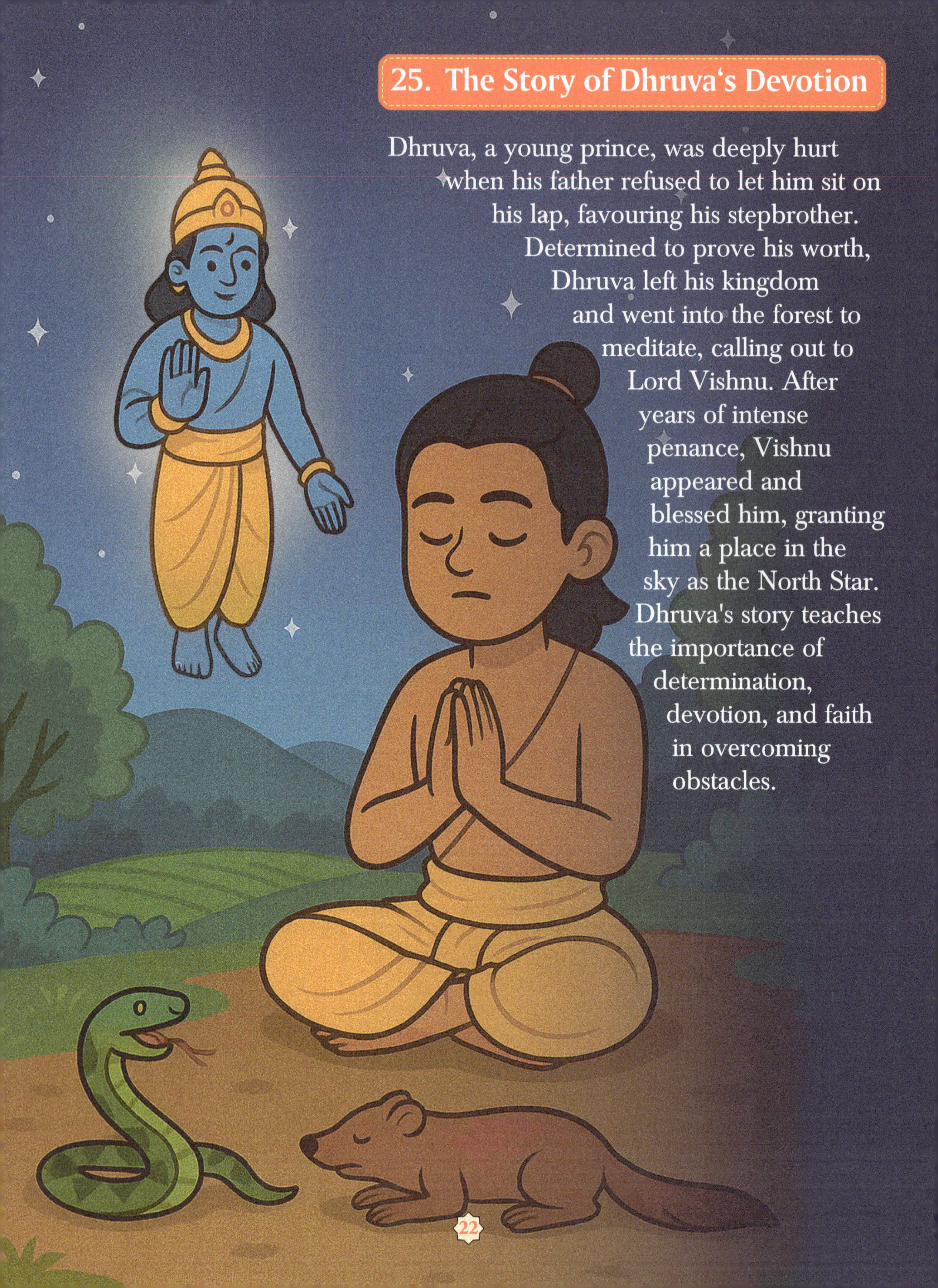

26. The Story of Arjuna and the Bhagavad Gita

On the battlefield of Kurukshetra, Arjuna, the mighty warrior, was filled with doubt and sorrow as he faced the prospect of fighting his own relatives. Lord Krishna, his charioteer, counseled him in the form of the *Bhagavad Gita*, a spiritual dialogue. Krishna taught Arjuna about duty, righteousness, and the nature of life and death. Arjuna, guided by Krishna's wisdom, overcame his inner conflict and decided to fulfill his duty, ultimately winning the war. This story highlights the importance of inner strength and spiritual guidance.

27. The Story of the Eagle Garuda

Garuda, the mighty eagle, was once the vehicle of Lord Vishnu. He was born of the union of Vinata and the sage Kashyapa, and from a young age, he exhibited immense strength and speed. When his mother was captured by the serpents, Garuda vowed to free her. He fought the serpents, defeating them and bringing back the *amrita* to save his mother. His story symbolises loyalty, strength, and the triumph of good over evil.

28. The Story of Vritra and Indra

Vritra, a fearsome demon, had taken control of the waters and imprisoned them in the mountains, causing drought and suffering. The gods called upon Indra, the king of the gods, to defeat him. Indra, armed with the thunderbolt *Vajra*, battled Vritra for days. Finally, with a mighty strike, Indra killed Vritra and released the waters, bringing life back to the earth. This story symbolises the triumph of good over evil and the restoration of balance in the world.

29. The Story of the Divine Swan

Once, Sage Brahma created a divine swan named Hamsa, who could separate the truth from falsehood with its divine wisdom. Hamsa's role was to assist the gods in discerning the essence of life. It would often fly between heaven and earth, imparting wisdom to those who sought it. The swan symbolises the eternal quest for knowledge, wisdom, and the power of discernment.

30. The Story of Satyavati

Satyavati was a fisherwoman who, through her extraordinary beauty and virtue, became the queen of the great King Shantanu. Before their marriage, Satyavati was sought after by Sage Parashara, who granted her the boon of bearing a famous child. Her son, Vyasa, became the author of the Mahabharata. Satyavati's story speaks of destiny, love, and sacrifice, showing how a humble life can lead to a significant role in shaping the future.

31. The Story of the Cursed Sage

Vishwamitra, once a powerful king, became a sage after his kingdom was taken from him. He meditated intensely to attain the status of Brahmarshi, the highest honour for a sage. However, his devotion was tested many times. Once, the beautiful Apsara Menaka tried to seduce him to break his penance, but Vishwamitra, with great determination, remained unaffected. His persistence and dedication to righteousness led him to become one of the greatest sages in Hindu mythology.

32. The Story of Shabari's Berries

Shabari was an elderly woman who lived in a remote forest. She had always dreamed of offering sweet berries to Lord Rama. After years of waiting, one day, Lord Rama visited her humble home. Shabari offered him the berries, which she had tasted herself to ensure they were sweet. Rama, deeply touched by her devotion and simplicity, ate the berries, and her life was blessed. This story teaches that true devotion does not lie in grandeur but in sincerity and love.

33. The Story of Lord Rama and the Golden Deer

During his exile, Lord Rama, along with Sita and Lakshmana, lived peacefully in the forest. One day, a golden deer appeared before them, and Sita asked Rama to capture it. Rama, though hesitant, set out to catch the deer. As he chased it, the deer led him away, and in his absence, Ravana abducted Sita. The golden deer was actually a disguise of Ravana's demon, Maricha. This event set the stage for the battle that would eventually rescue Sita.

34. The Story of The Sage's Curse

Ahalya, the beautiful wife of Sage Gautama, was once seduced by Lord Indra in the form of her husband. When Gautama discovered the betrayal, he cursed Ahalya to become a stone. A long time later, Lord Rama, during his travels, touched the stone with his foot, breaking the curse. Ahalya was restored to her human form. This story is a reflection on sin, repentance, and redemption, emphasising the power of divine intervention.

35. The Story of the Divine Vision

During the Kurukshetra war, Lord Krishna granted Arjuna divine vision to witness the cosmic form of the Supreme God. As Arjuna gazed upon Krishna's universal form, he saw countless beings and gods, the past, present, and future, all within Krishna's body. Arjuna was awestruck and overwhelmed by the sight. This moment symbolises the realisation of the infinite nature of the divine and the deeper understanding of reality beyond human perception.

36. The Story of the Sage and the Lion

Once, a great sage named Vishvamitra meditated for years to attain spiritual power. One day, a mighty lion appeared in his ashram, threatening to devour him. The sage, calm and unafraid, simply stared at the lion and spoke a mantra. Instantly, the lion became docile and sat peacefully beside the sage. This story highlights the power of meditation and spiritual energy in overcoming even the fiercest challenges.

37. The Story of the Curse of Mandodari

Mandodari, the wife of Ravana, was a wise and noble queen. When her husband abducted Sita, she tried to stop him, advising him against the wrong he was doing. Ravana, blinded by his pride, ignored her. As Ravana's downfall approached, Mandodari, deeply sorrowed by the fate of her husband, cursed the land of Lanka to be destroyed by fire, symbolising how the consequences of bad actions lead to irreversible outcomes.

38. The Story of King Vikramaditya's Justice

King Vikramaditya, known for his wisdom and fairness, was once challenged by a demon who demanded that he tell a story of justice in order to pass. Vikramaditya narrated a story about a prince who showed mercy to a man who had wronged him, believing that true justice lies not in punishment but in the opportunity for reform. The demon, impressed by the king's wisdom, allowed him to pass. This tale underscores the importance of compassion and fairness in leadership.

39. The Story of the Birth of Hanuman

Anjana, a celestial nymph, was blessed by Lord Shiva with a son who would be a great devotee of Lord Rama. She prayed fervently, and as a result, Hanuman was born with extraordinary powers. His immense strength and devotion made him an indispensable ally in Rama's battle against Ravana. Hanuman's birth story symbolises divine blessings, the power of devotion, and the strength that comes from spiritual dedication.

40. The Story of the Three Boons

King Dasharatha, the father of Lord Rama, once granted three boons to his wife Kaikeyi, who had helped him in battle. However, Kaikeyi, swayed by her maid, asked Dasharatha to fulfill two of those boons: banishing Rama to the forest and making her own son, Bharata, the king. Though heartbroken, Dasharatha honoured his promise. This tale speaks of the weight of promises and the unforeseen consequences of selfish desires.

41. The Story of King Harishchandra's Sacrifice

King Harishchandra was known for his unwavering commitment to truth and justice. One day, Sage Vishwamitra tested his devotion by causing him immense suffering. Harishchandra lost his kingdom, wealth, and family but remained steadfast in his commitment to truth. Finally, when his wife was sold as a servant, Harishchandra himself worked as a cremator to earn his living. His ultimate sacrifice was rewarded when the gods restored his kingdom, showing that truth and integrity prevail despite trials.

42. The Story of the Brahmastra

The Brahmastra was a powerful weapon created by Lord Brahma, capable of destroying entire worlds. Arjuna, a skilled archer, was given the weapon by Lord Shiva during his travels. It was said that once released, the Brahmastra could not be stopped. However, it was used only in dire circumstances, symbolising the immense responsibility that comes with power. The story of the Brahmastra teaches the importance of wisdom and restraint when wielding great power.

43. The Story of Nandi's Loyalty

Nandi, the divine bull, is the loyal mount of Lord Shiva. Once, when Lord Shiva was deep in meditation, Nandi protected him from the disturbance of a group of demons. Despite being outnumbered, Nandi fought valiantly, ensuring that Lord Shiva's meditation was uninterrupted. Nandi's loyalty to his lord symbolises the ideal of selfless devotion and the importance of protecting sacred duties at all costs.

44. The Story of Rishi Durvasa and the Curse of Indra

Rishi Durvasa, known for his fiery temper, once gave a divine garland to King Indra as a gift. Indra, however, became prideful and did not show the proper respect. In anger, Durvasa cursed Indra, saying that the heavens would be devoid of all their powers and riches. This curse led to the *Churning of the Ocean*, where the gods and demons worked together to obtain the nectar of immortality, *amrita*, to restore their lost strength. This story illustrates how humility is vital in maintaining power.

45. The Story of Goddess Durga's Battle with Mahishasura

Mahishasura, a demon, had gained a boon that made him invincible to all male gods. To defeat him, the gods created Goddess Durga, a powerful manifestation of all their combined powers. Riding a lion, Durga battled Mahishasura for days, finally slaying him and restoring peace to the world. Durga's victory over Mahishasura is celebrated during the festival of Durga Puja and symbolises the triumph of good over evil.

46. The Story of Ravana's Wisdom and His Downfall

Ravana, the demon king of Lanka, was not just a great warrior, but also a scholar and devotee of Lord Shiva. His devotion earned him the powerful boon of invincibility. However, his arrogance led him to abduct Sita, which set the stage for his ultimate downfall. Despite his wisdom, Ravana's pride and disregard for righteousness led to his destruction, teaching that knowledge and power must always be accompanied by humility and respect for others.

47. The Story of the Divine Twins

The Ashwini Kumars were twin gods of medicine, known for their healing powers and beauty. Born to the sun god Surya and his wife Saranyu, they were skilled in treating both gods and mortals. One day, they rescued a king who had been cursed by a sage and healed him. Their story highlights the importance of health and the healing arts, as well as the value of compassion and care for others.

48. The Story of Prahlad's Devotion to Lord Vishnu

Prahlad, the son of the demon king Hiranyakashipu, was a staunch devotee of Lord Vishnu. His father, who despised Vishnu, tried repeatedly to make Prahlad abandon his devotion, but Prahlad's faith remained unshaken. Hiranyakashipu attempted to kill his son several times, but each time,

Vishnu miraculously protected Prahlad. Eventually, Vishnu incarnated as Narasimha, a half-man, half-lion, to kill Hiranyakashipu and protect his devoted follower. This story emphasises the power of unwavering devotion.

49. The Story of the Birth of Lord Kartikeya

Lord Kartikeya, the god of war, was born from the union of Lord Shiva and Parvati. He was created to defeat the demon Tarakasura, who had terrorised the heavens. Kartikeya grew up to be a formidable warrior and led the divine army against Tarakasura, defeating him in a great battle. Kartikeya's story highlights the importance of valour and duty, as well as the divine intervention that occurs when evil threatens the peace of the world.

50. The Story of Sage Agastya and the Southern Seas

Sage Agastya, one of the great rishis of Hindu mythology, was once instructed to move south to balance the weight of the earth. He and his wife, Lopamudra, journeyed southward, where they drank up the waters of the southern seas to ensure the land would not flood. Agastya's story highlights his immense power, wisdom, and role in maintaining cosmic balance. He is also credited with many of the hymns in the *Rigveda*.

51. The Story of the Birth of Lakshmi

Lakshmi, the goddess of wealth and prosperity, was born from the churning of the ocean, the result of the great *Samudra Manthan* between the gods and demons. As the nectar of immortality emerged, so did Lakshmi, radiant and beautiful. She chose Lord Vishnu as her eternal consort, and together they ruled over wealth and fortune. Lakshmi's birth reminds us of the importance of wealth, not just in material terms but in terms of wisdom, virtue, and blessings.

52. The Story of Draupadi's Birth

Draupadi, the wife of the five Pandavas, was born from the fire during a yajna performed by King Drupada. As she emerged from the flames, she was a symbol of purity and strength. Her birth was a divine intervention, and it was foretold that she would play a key role in the destruction of the Kauravas. Draupadi's story is one of resilience, devotion, and unwavering righteousness, as she stood against injustice during the Mahabharata.

53. The Story of Sage Bhrigu and His Test of the Gods

Sage Bhrigu once decided to test the three main gods of the Hindu pantheon—Brahma, Vishnu, and Shiva—to see who was the most worthy of devotion. First, he went to Brahma, who treated him coldly. Next, he approached Lord Shiva, who welcomed him warmly but did not recognise his anger. Finally, Bhrigu visited Lord Vishnu, who, despite having been insulted, simply lay down to rest with a smile, offering Bhrigu his feet. Impressed by Vishnu's humility, Bhrigu declared him the greatest of all gods.

54. The Story of the Churning of the Ocean

In the quest for the nectar of immortality, the gods and demons decided to churn the ocean (samudra manthan). Mount Mandara was used as the churning rod, and the serpent Vasuki as the rope. As they churned, numerous treasures emerged, including the goddess Lakshmi, the moon, and the *amrita* (nectar of immortality). However, when the poison *halahala* emerged, Lord Shiva drank it to save the world, his throat turning blue. This event is the origin of the festival of Maha Shivaratri.

55. The Story of Bhima's Oath Against Duryodhana

During the Mahabharata war, Bhima, the second Pandava, vowed to avenge the insults and wrongdoings of Duryodhana, the eldest of the Kauravas. When Duryodhana humiliated Draupadi, Bhima swore to break his thigh in the battle. During the war, Bhima fulfilled his vow and crushed Duryodhana's thigh with a powerful blow, fulfilling his promise. This story highlights the importance of justice and the power of vows made in the name of righteousness.

56. The Story of the Mahabharata Dice Game

The Mahabharata includes a pivotal moment where Yudhishthira, the eldest Pandava, was tricked into gambling away his kingdom, brothers, and even himself. The game was a setup by the Kauravas, leading to the Pandavas' exile. Draupadi, who was humiliated during this game, called upon Lord Krishna for help. Krishna, ever the protector of righteousness, ensured that Draupadi was saved. This story is a lesson in the dangers of pride, manipulation, and the importance of dharma.

57. The Story of the Sage's Test

Nachiketa, a young boy, once sought to understand the secret of life and death. In his search, he went to the god of death, Yama, and asked him to reveal the ultimate truth. Yama, impressed by his courage and wisdom, granted him three wishes. The first two were material, but for the third wish, Nachiketa asked about the nature of life after death. Yama imparted deep philosophical wisdom to him, showing that true knowledge transcends the physical world and is the key to liberation.

58. The Story of Kacha and Devayani

Kacha, the son of Sage Shukra, once went to learn the secret of reviving the dead from Devayani, the daughter of Sage Shukra. Devayani fell in love with him, but Kacha, bound by his duties as a student, did not reciprocate. After a series of trials and tribulations, Kacha was killed by Devayani's stepmother, Sharmishtha, but was revived by the magic of his guru. Eventually, Kacha revealed the secrets of the elixir of life, and Devayani's love remained unfulfilled. This tale speaks of loyalty, duty, and the pursuit of knowledge.

59. The Story of Vali and Sugriva

Vali and Sugriva were brothers and the rulers of the Vanara kingdom. After a dispute, Vali drove Sugriva out of the kingdom. Sugriva later allied with Lord Rama to defeat Vali. When Rama shot Vali in the heart, Vali's dying words expressed the injustice of his brother's exile. Rama explained that he had killed Vali for justice, as Vali had wronged his brother. The story speaks of loyalty, justice, and the complexity of relationships.

60. The Story of Sage Kapila and the Sons of Sagara

King Sagara had performed a great sacrifice, but his sons were cursed by Sage Kapila. The curse led to their destruction, and their souls could not ascend to heaven. The curse could only be broken by the arrival of Lord Rama. When Rama's foot touched the ashes of the sons of Sagara, their souls were freed, and they ascended to heaven. This story emphasises the importance of piety, sacrifice, and the influence of divine intervention.

61. The Story of the Rajaswala and King Yayati

King Yayati, after being cursed with old age by the sage Shukracharya, sought to regain his youth. His sons, Yadu, and Druhyu, each refused to exchange their youth for his old age, except for his son, Puru. However, after receiving youth, Yayati became selfish and continued his indulgent life. Eventually, realising his mistakes, he returned the youth to Puru, thereby understanding that material indulgence could not satisfy true happiness. This story teaches the consequences of greed and the importance of self-control.

62. The Story of the Creation of the Gayatri Mantra

Sage Vishwamitra, once a king, gave up his throne and embarked on a rigorous path of meditation to attain the status of a Brahmarishi. He underwent great hardships, facing challenges from the demons and gods. After many years of penance, Vishwamitra received the sacred Gayatri Mantra from Lord Brahma, a mantra that bestows wisdom and protection. This story highlights the power of dedication and the ability to transform one's fate through devotion.

63. The Story of the Saving of the Vedas by Lord Shiva

Once, when the Vedas were in danger of being lost during a cosmic event, Lord Shiva took the form of a sage and protected them. As the gods and demons fought over the Vedas, Shiva intervened and ensured that they remained safe for the future of humanity. This story signifies the importance of knowledge, wisdom, and the divine protection that ensures the preservation of sacred teachings.

64. The Story of the Creation of the Big Dipper

The seven great rishis—Vashistha, Atri, Bharadwaja, Gautama, Vishwamitra, Jamadagni, and Kanva—were revered for their wisdom and penance. They are believed to have ascended to the heavens and become the stars in the constellation of the Big Dipper, which can be seen in the northern sky. Their story highlights the importance of knowledge, virtue, and spiritual dedication. The seven rishis' sacrifice and wisdom continue to inspire generations.

65. The Story of Ganesha and the Race Around the World

Once, Sage Narada gave a magical fruit of knowledge to Lord Shiva and Parvati and said it should be given to only one of their sons—Ganesha or Kartikeya. To decide, Shiva proposed a race around the world. Kartikeya sped off on his peacock, flying across mountains and oceans. But Ganesha simply circled his parents three times and said, "You are my whole world." Touched by his wisdom, Shiva and Parvati gave him the fruit.

66. The Story of the Birth of Ashwatthama

Ashwatthama, the son of Dronacharya, was born with a gem embedded in his forehead, making him invincible. His birth was a boon from Lord Shiva to Drona, who had prayed for an extraordinary son. Ashwatthama's gem protected him from disease and fear. Later, his obsession with revenge during the Mahabharata war led to tragic consequences, but his birth remains a tale of divine blessing and unique destiny.

67. The Story of Ganesha's Broken Tusk

When Sage Vyasa needed someone to write the epic Mahabharata, Lord Ganesha offered to do so on one condition: Vyasa must not pause while reciting. In return, Vyasa demanded Ganesha only write if he fully understood the verses. Midway, Ganesha's pen broke, and he broke his own tusk to continue. This story explains why Ganesha is also called Ekadanta, the one-tusked deity.

68. The Story of Sage Markandeya

Sage Markandeya was destined to die young. However, his unwavering devotion to Lord Shiva saved him. On his death day, Yama, the god of death, approached to take his life. Markandeya clung to a Shiva Lingam and prayed. Lord Shiva appeared and defeated Yama, granting Markandeya eternal life. This story emphasises the power of devotion and divine grace.

69. The Story of Arjuna's Penance

To obtain the Pashupatastra, a powerful weapon, Arjuna performed severe penance to please Lord Shiva. Shiva appeared in the guise of a hunter and tested Arjuna's skills in battle. Satisfied with his determination and skill, Shiva revealed his true form and granted Arjuna the weapon. This tale highlights dedication and the rewards of perseverance.

70. The Story of King Trishanku

King Trishanku desired to ascend to heaven in his mortal body. Sage Vishwamitra agreed to help him, but the gods rejected this unusual wish. In anger, Vishwamitra created a parallel heaven for Trishanku, hanging him in mid-air between earth and heaven. This story showcases the limits of ambition and the power of a sage's will.

71. The Story of Mandodari's Wisdom

Mandodari, the wife of Ravana, was known for her wisdom and grace. She repeatedly warned Ravana against abducting Sita and facing Lord Rama's wrath. Her advice went unheeded, leading to the fall of Lanka. Mandodari's story is a reminder of the importance of listening to wise counsel.

72. The Story of the Vanara King Vriksharaja

Vriksharaja, a Vanara king, helped Rama by providing the resources and assistance needed to build the bridge to Lanka. His massive forest was cut down to construct the bridge. Vriksharaja's story is a testament to sacrifice and collaboration for a greater cause.

73. The Story of Matsyendra

Lord Shiva once imparted secret knowledge of yoga to Parvati. A fish nearby overheard their conversation. Shiva, recognising the fish's devotion, blessed it to take human form as Matsyendra, the founder of Hatha Yoga. Matsyendra became a revered yogi and teacher, spreading the divine knowledge.

74. The Birth of Kumbhakarna

Ravana's brother, Kumbhakarna, was immensely strong but cursed to sleep for six months at a time. During a boon-granting ceremony, he intended to ask for "Indrasana" (the throne of Indra), but his tongue was tied by Saraswati, causing him to say "Nidrasana" (bed of sleep). This mishap saved the gods from his constant wrath.

75. The Story of the Syamantaka Jewel

The Syamantaka Jewel, owned by King Satrajit, was said to bring immense wealth but also invited greed and conflict. When the jewel went missing, Lord Krishna was falsely accused of theft. To clear his name, Krishna tracked down the jewel, slayed a lion, and returned it to its rightful owner, symbolising the triumph of truth.

76. The Birth of Karna

Karna, the son of Kunti and the sun god Surya, was born with golden armor and earrings. Abandoned by Kunti due to her unwed status, he was raised by a charioteer. Despite his hardships, Karna became a legendary warrior, embodying loyalty and valour, though his tragic fate reflects the complex nature of dharma.

77. The Story of Mandhata

King Mandhata was born from the union of Sage Yuvanashva and the water of a sacred vessel blessed by the gods. Raised by celestial beings, Mandhata grew into a just and powerful king. His tale highlights divine intervention in preserving righteousness.

78. The Boar Avatar (Varaha)

In the form of a boar, Lord Vishnu descended as Varaha to rescue the earth, which had been submerged in the cosmic ocean by the demon Hiranyaksha. Vishnu lifted the earth with his tusks and defeated the demon, restoring balance to the universe. This story symbolises the protection of dharma against chaos.

79. The Legend of Nala and Damayanti

Nala, a virtuous king, and Damayanti, a princess, were united by love. However, due to a divine game of dice manipulated by Kali, Nala lost his kingdom and was separated from Damayanti. After enduring numerous trials, their unwavering love and devotion brought them back together. This tale symbolises perseverance through adversity.

80. The Curse of Chyavana

Sage Chyavana, disturbed by King Sharyati's soldiers, cursed them to fall ill. The king sought forgiveness, offering his daughter Sukanya in marriage. Chyavana's gratitude to Sukanya led him to regain his youth, with divine aid from the Ashwini twins. This story highlights the transformative power of love.

81. The Theft of Vedas by Hayagriva

Hayagriva, a demon, stole the sacred Vedas from Brahma, plunging the world into ignorance. Lord Vishnu, assuming the form of a fish (Matsya), retrieved the Vedas, restoring cosmic knowledge. This tale emphasises Vishnu's role as the preserver of wisdom.

82. The Legend of Savitri and Satyavan

Savitri, a devoted wife, defied Yama, the god of death, when he took her husband, Satyavan. Her wisdom and persistence impressed Yama, who granted Satyavan's life back. This story showcases the strength of marital devotion and the triumph of determination.

83. The Curse of Urvashi on Arjuna

During his exile, Arjuna rejected the advances of Urvashi, a celestial nymph. Angered, she cursed him to lose his manhood. This curse later became a boon when Arjuna lived incognito as a eunuch during the Pandavas' year of anonymity. This tale illustrates the interplay of curses and blessings.

84. The Creation of the Kauravas

The Kauravas were born to Gandhari through an extraordinary process. Her impatience with a prolonged pregnancy led her to strike her womb, resulting in a hundred pieces. These pieces were nurtured in jars, giving birth to the hundred Kauravas. This story reflects the unusual origins of the epic's central antagonists.

85. The Birth of Lakshmana Rekha

When Sita was abducted by Ravana, Lakshmana drew a protective line around their hut, forbidding her from crossing it. This Lakshmana Rekha became a symbol of boundaries, caution, and protection in Indian culture. The tale warns against yielding to temptation.

86. The Story of Vibheeshana's Defection

Vibheeshana, Ravana's righteous brother, tried to dissuade him from waging war against Rama. When Ravana refused, Vibheeshana joined Rama's side, valuing dharma over familial loyalty. This tale highlights the moral strength to uphold righteousness.

87. The Curse of the Gandharva Angaraparana

Arjuna once defeated Angaraparana, a celestial being, during the Pandavas' exile. In return, Angaraparana cursed Arjuna that he would struggle to recognise his true allies. This story emphasises the unforeseen consequences of one's actions.

88. The Birth of the Maruts

When Diti, mother of the demons, sought a son to defeat the gods, Indra tricked her by prematurely cutting her womb. The pieces transformed into the Maruts, storm deities who became allies of Indra. This tale demonstrates how divine intervention maintains cosmic order.

89. The Tale of Shunashepa

Shunashepa, a sage's son, was chosen as a sacrificial offering by King Harishchandra to appease the gods. In his desperate plea, Shunashepa recited prayers to Lord Indra and Varuna, who saved him.

His story illustrates the power of sincere devotion in overcoming dire circumstances.

90. The Curse of Nalakuvara and Manigriva

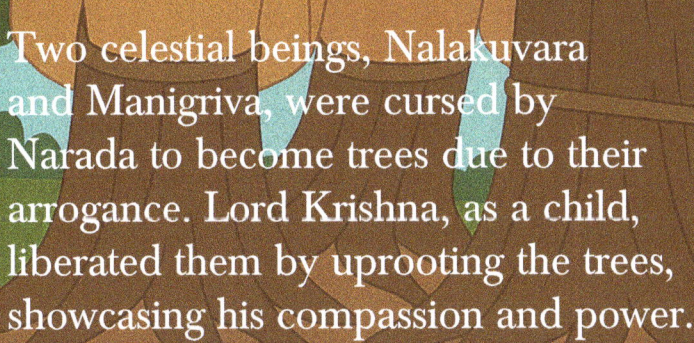

Two celestial beings, Nalakuvara and Manigriva, were cursed by Narada to become trees due to their arrogance. Lord Krishna, as a child, liberated them by uprooting the trees, showcasing his compassion and power.

91. The Story of Uloopi and Arjuna

Uloopi, a Naga princess, fell in love with Arjuna and revived him using her mystic powers after he was cursed by the Ganga. Arjun then married Uloopi. She later helped him during the Kurukshetra war. Her story highlights loyalty and devotion.

92. The Story of Chudala and Sikhidhvaja

Queen Chudala, disguised as a sage, guided her husband Sikhidhvaja towards self-realisation when he renounced the throne for asceticism. Her wisdom and dedication illustrate the transformative power of true love and spiritual understanding.

93. The Ascent of Trishira

Trishira was a strong demon with three heads! Ravana created him to fight the gods. Trishira thought he was unbeatable and tried to take over the heavens. But he was too proud. Lord Indra, the king of the gods, fought back bravely. With a flash of lightning, Indra defeated Trishira. The gods celebrated! This story teaches that being proud and mean never ends well—even if you're super strong. Kindness and respect are always better than arrogance.

94. The Creation of Chaturvani

Lord Brahma, the creator, wanted everyone in the universe to talk and share ideas. So, he made four types of speech called Chaturvani. The first is Para, which is quiet thought. The second is Pashyanti, where words start to form. The third is Madhyama, the voice in your mind. The last is Vaikhari, which is what you speak out loud! Brahma's gift helped people understand one another. This story reminds us that words are powerful and should be used kindly and wisely.

95. The Legend of Swetaketu

Swetaketu was a smart boy who learned the Vedas quickly. But soon, he became too proud and thought he knew everything! His father asked him, "Do you know what helps you understand everything?" Swetaketu didn't know. He realised he still had a lot to learn. So, he studied harder and became wiser and more humble. This story teaches that being smart is good—but being humble is even better. There's always something new to learn!

96. The Curse of Shringi on King Parikshit

One day, King Parikshit was tired and thirsty. He entered a sage's home, but the sage was meditating and didn't answer. Angry, the king put a dead snake around the sage's neck. The sage's son, Shringi, was upset and cursed the king to die in seven days by a snake bite! The king felt sorry and spent his last days listening to stories of the gods. He accepted his fate calmly. This story teaches that we should always be respectful and that everyone—even kings—must face the results of their actions.

97. The Tale of Rishyashringa

Queen Chudala was wise and kind. She found peace through meditation and tried to teach her husband, King Sikhidhvaja. But he didn't believe her and left to live in the forest as a hermit. Chudala dressed as a wise sage and followed him. Slowly, she helped him learn about true peace and happiness. When he realised the sage was actually his wife, he also understood her wisdom. This story shows that anyone—man or woman—can be wise, and true love means helping each other grow.

98. The Destruction of Tripura

Long ago, three evil demon brothers built magical flying cities called
Tripura. No one could stop them—they were too powerful! But the cities
lined up in the sky only once in a thousand years. Lord Shiva waited for
that perfect moment. When the cities aligned, he shot a single arrow and
destroyed them all at once! Everyone cheered as peace returned. This story
shows how Lord Shiva uses his power to protect the world and defeat evil
when the time is right.

99. The Boon of King Muchukunda

King Muchukunda, a devout ruler, assisted the gods in their wars against demons. As a reward, he was granted the boon of eternal sleep, with a curse that anyone who disturbed him would be burned to ashes. Muchukunda later awakened to destroy a demon, illustrating how divine justice works through unexpected means.

100. The Story of King Kakudmi

King Kakudmi and his daughter Revati sought Lord Brahma's advice on choosing a husband for her. Time passed differently in Brahma's realm, and upon their return, they found ages had passed on Earth. Revati eventually married Balarama, Krishna's brother, highlighting the relativity of time in divine realms.

101. The Curse of Nahusha

Nahusha, a mortal king, was temporarily made the king of heaven. However, his arrogance grew, and he disrespected Sage Agastya. As a result, Agastya cursed Nahusha to turn into a serpent and live on Earth until liberated by the Pandavas. This story emphasises the dangers of pride.